WHEN THE GERMIES ARE GONE

Written by Bran Middlederth
Illustrated by Nico Adi Surya P.W.

www.germiesbook.com

When the germies are gone
I'll have so much fun.

I'll play and spend days wherever I want.

I'll invade the arcade.

Start my own parade.

I'll even behave
at the restaurant.

When the germies are over,
I'll save masks for October.

Trick or treat down the street
as a big, smelly ogre.

Some days I can't decide
if it's afternoon or night.

My body fills with sleepy gloom
missing normal life.

Other times my legs will twitch.
I feel this crazy jittery-ness.

They need to move.
But they're stuck in grooves
of weird, invisible stickiness.

The inside life isn't just sad drama.
There's bedside climbs,
when the floor is made of lava.

Adventures at night,
like a pajama saga.

We go outside for bike rides,
bubbles, and java.

When the germies are finally done,
we'll host game night for once.

And remember these times
we can look back upon...

Like some wobbly merry-go-round we rode on.

Sometimes we danced.
Sometimes we just held on.

I'll sing and I'll dream,
and love all of the minutes.

I'll skip and I'll twirl.

I'll high-five the world.

I'll say HEEEYYY!!!
TODAY is a DARN GOOD DAY to exist!

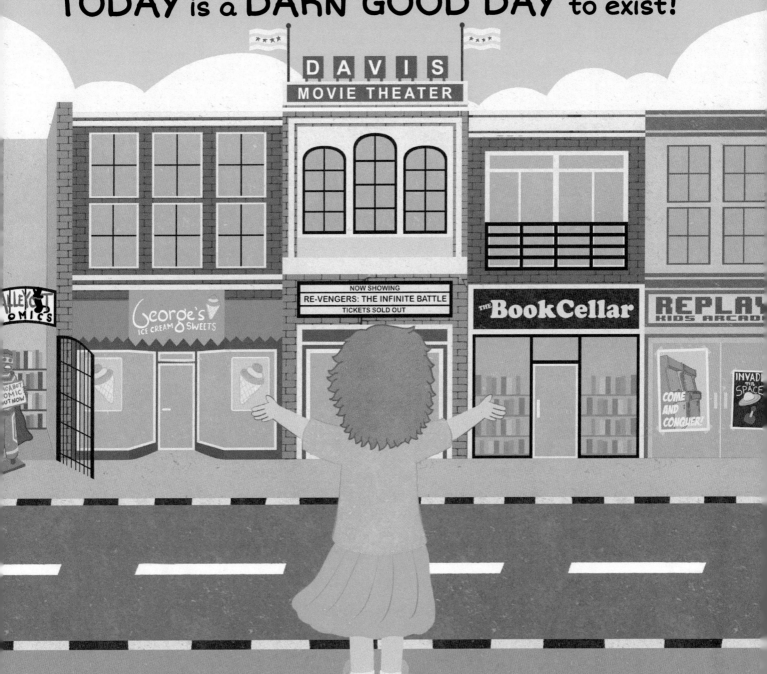

I'll play and spend days
wherever I want.

Made in the USA
Middletown, DE
22 August 2021